My Little Pony

Under the Sparkling Sea

Mary Jane Begin

Little, Brown and Company

New York • Boston

This book was edited by Marissa Mansolillo and Erin Stein and designed by Mary Jane Begin and Steve Scott. The logo treatment was created by Chris Allio. The production was supervised by Charlotte Veaney, and the production editor was Christine Ma. A special thank you to Ed Lane. • The illustrations for this book were created as mixed-media paintings on Canson pastel paper. The text was set in ITC Barcelona, and the display types are Mishka and Pepito. The pages were printed on 128 gsm Gold Sun Matte.

First Edition: April 2013

Library of Congress Cataloging-in-Publication Data

Begin, Mary Jane.
Under the Sparkling Sea / Mary Jane Begin.—1st ed.
p. cm.—(My little pony)
Summary: "The ponies travel to the underwater world of Aquastria"—Provided by publisher.
ISBN 978-0-316-24559-3
I. Title.
PZ7.B388216Und 2013
(Fic)—dc23   2012040749

10 9 8 7 6 5 4 3 2 1 • LEO • Printed in China

I dedicate this book to a wild imaginative spirit
and my dear pony friends:

Theresa ~ Fluttershy

Anneka ~ Rarity

Linda ~ Twilight Sparkle

Freda ~ Rainbow Dash

Krista ~ Applejack

Marissa ~ Pinkie Pie

Mom ~ Princess Celestia

A special invitation arrived at Golden Oak Library in Ponyville.

"It's here! It's finally here!" cried Twilight Sparkle as she opened the shimmering envelope. She began reading the invitation out loud to Spike, a young dragon who was her best first assistant at the library.

The pleasure of your company is requested at the Annual Aquastria Race. Attendants and friends are welcome. The race will officially begin after the First Moon Tide.

Very truly yours,
King Leo,
Ruler of Aquastria

"Isn't Aquastria...you know, *underwater*?" asked Spike.
"*Of course* it's underwater!" said Twilight.

Twilight asked her friends Rarity, Applejack, Pinkie Pie, Rainbow Dash, and Fluttershy to come with her and Spike to Aquastria.

"Watch," explained Twilight. "I'll cast a spell that gives you special magical gills so you can breathe underwater like fish, and fins so you can swim faster."

Her unicorn horn glowed, and it was done.

"Hmmm," said Rarity, waggling her fins. "I don't like getting my mane wet!"

"Call me a landlubber, but I'd rather keep my hooves on solid ground!" declared Applejack.

"Is there a party? You can count me in!" cried Pinkie Pie. "I wonder what happens to balloons underwater."

"How will I fly with wet wings?" grumbled Rainbow Dash.

"I think it sounds like fun," Fluttershy whispered softly. "I'd love to meet our cousins, the seaponies!"

Twilight Sparkle insisted that the trip would be the grandest adventure ever, and after lots of convincing, she finally won over her friends.

There was just one more thing to do before the trip. The spell for magic gills didn't work on dragons.

"Here, Spike, you'll need to wear this helmet so you can breathe," she said.

Spike looked at the glass bubble, folded his arms, and shook his head. "I'm definitely not wearing that thing. Nope. Not wearing it."

"You have to wear it if you want to come with us," insisted Twilight.

Spike shook his head. "No *way*."

Twilight stuck it on his head with a quick *plunk*!

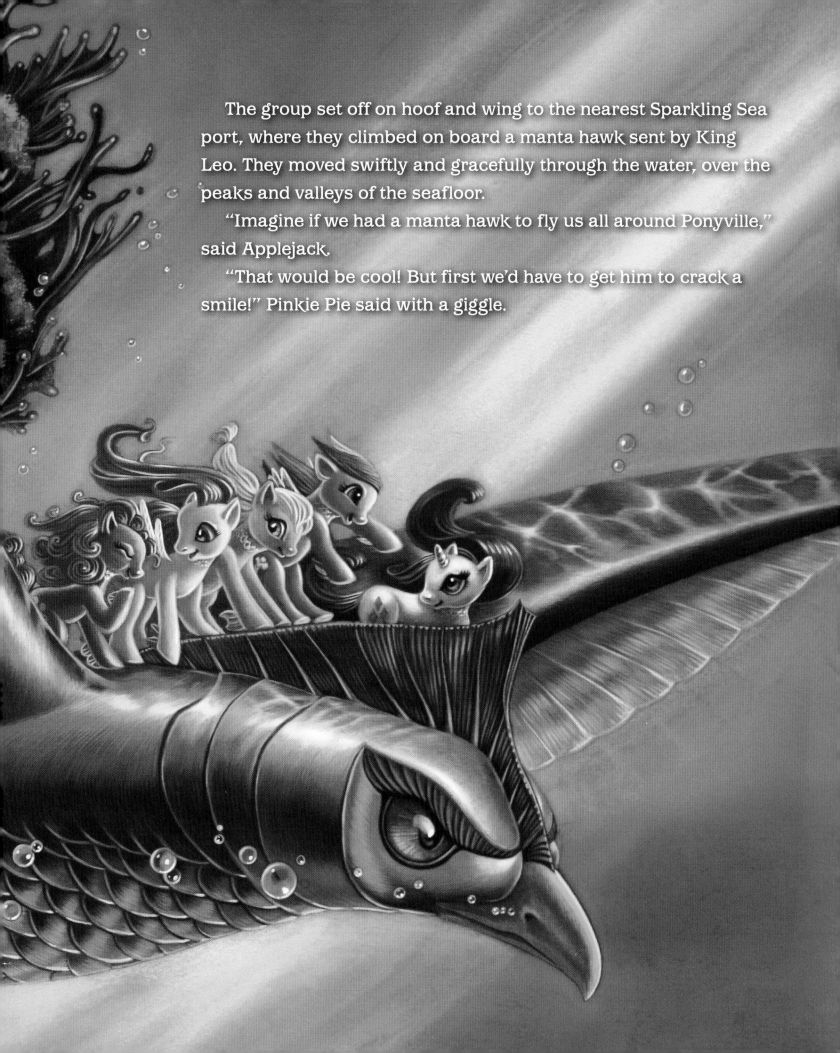

The group set off on hoof and wing to the nearest Sparkling Sea port, where they climbed on board a manta hawk sent by King Leo. They moved swiftly and gracefully through the water, over the peaks and valleys of the seafloor.

"Imagine if we had a manta hawk to fly us all around Ponyville," said Applejack.

"That would be cool! But first we'd have to get him to crack a smile!" Pinkie Pie said with a giggle.

When they reached Aquastria, two seaponies
met them at the entrance to a beautiful seashell
structure known as Nautilus Hall.

"It's great to see you, Twilight
Sparkle! And to meet more of our
cousins from Equestria!" said Coral,
an orange-striped seapony.

"This is my brother, Arrow," she added,
gesturing with her fin. "Come with us to
Nautilus Hall and meet King Leo, the leader
of Aquastria."

"We'll introduce you to the mermares,
too, *if* they're feeling friendly," said Arrow
with a grin.

"Welcome, friends," said King Leo warmly. "You will stay with us here at Nautilus Hall as my honored guests."

The hall sparkled so brightly with sea crystals, spiraling shells, and shimmering lights that Rarity looked ready to faint. "It's fabulous!"

"Those lights are moving!" cried Pinkie Pie.

"Those are jellyflies," explained Arrow. "They light up all over Aquastria." Just then, a jellyfly landed on his head. The ponies laughed as the gentle creature floated away only to perch on Fluttershy's nose.

"Hi," she whispered shyly to the jellyfly.

The ponies were thrilled to spend the rest of the day with their cousins, the seaponies, who were a funny and friendly bunch. The mermares were a different matter; they kept to themselves.

"This is Electra," Coral said cautiously as one moved gracefully toward them. "She is one of the fastest mermares in the race."

"Nice to meet you!" exclaimed Rainbow Dash as she bolted up to the towering mermare and thrust out her hoof.

Electra flipped her tail and swam away at lightning speed.

"What did I say?" asked an embarrassed Rainbow Dash.

"It's okay," said Coral. "Mermares are very shy ... but I think she's curious about you. Wait until you see her race. . . . She's amazing!"

"And nearly impossible to beat," said Arrow with a sigh.

After a good night's sleep, the ponies were invited to explore Aquastria.

Rainbow Dash joined Coral at the Nautilus Stables and practiced swimming with the seaponies.

Applejack helped with the harvest of new seaweed at Oceanic Farm.

Curious to know what sweet treats were on the menu, Pinkie Pie offered to help the chefs at Nautilus Hall!

Rarity was given a sneak peek
of the Aquastrian
ceremonial costumes.

And Spike joined Twilight Sparkle and Fluttershy,
who were curious about the Sea Grass Forest.
The trio swam into the dense seaweed
to explore.

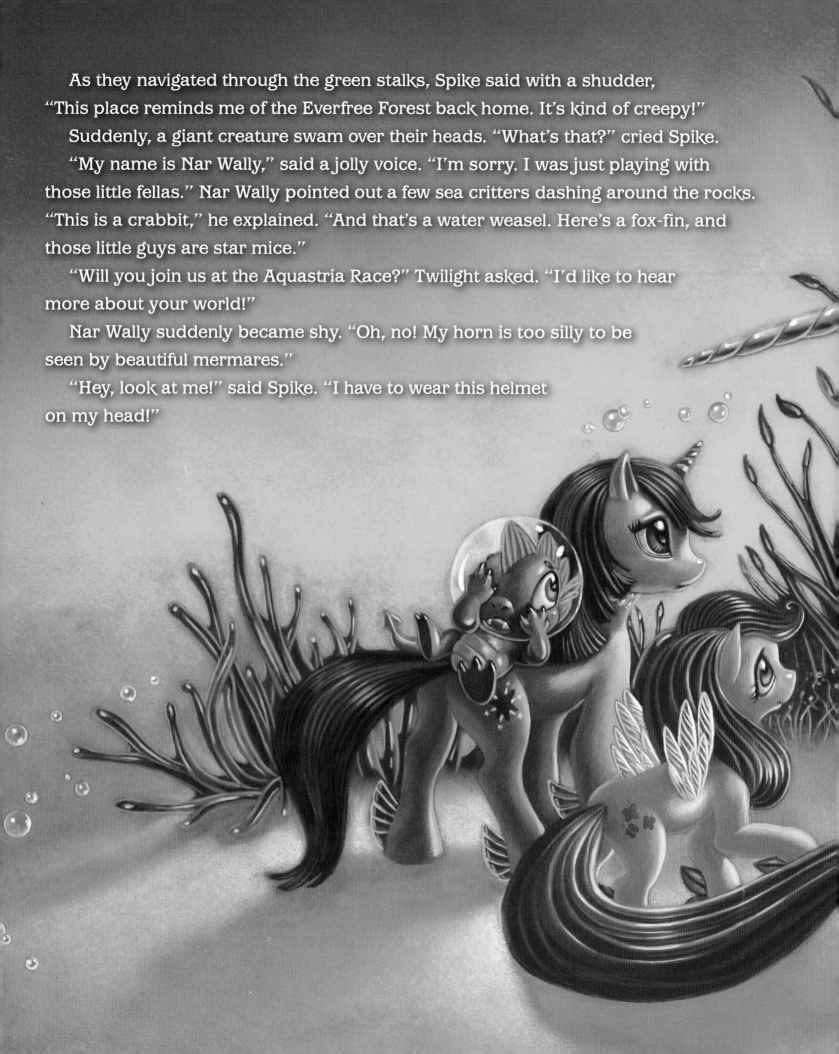

As they navigated through the green stalks, Spike said with a shudder, "This place reminds me of the Everfree Forest back home. It's kind of creepy!"

Suddenly, a giant creature swam over their heads. "What's that?" cried Spike.

"My name is Nar Wally," said a jolly voice. "I'm sorry. I was just playing with those little fellas." Nar Wally pointed out a few sea critters dashing around the rocks. "This is a crabbit," he explained. "And that's a water weasel. Here's a fox-fin, and those little guys are star mice."

"Will you join us at the Aquastria Race?" Twilight asked. "I'd like to hear more about your world!"

Nar Wally suddenly became shy. "Oh, no! My horn is too silly to be seen by beautiful mermares."

"Hey, look at me!" said Spike. "I have to wear this helmet on my head!"

"We'll tell you what it's like up on dry land,"
Fluttershy promised.

Nar Wally was so curious about his new friends
that he finally agreed to join them.

The group got to the race just in time to see the teams line up at the start.

"This is *so* exciting!" squealed Pinkie Pie.

"And dangerous..." said Applejack.

"It's exciting *and* dangerous, for sure," warned Twilight. "The teams have never raced through Crabbit's Canyon before. Speeding past craggy rocks and whirlpools won't be easy."

"Here's how the Annual Aquastria Race works," Rainbow Dash began. "Each team member has a turn in a different part of the race. After each part is completed, he or she passes a baton to the next teammate. The last one races toward the finish line and wins the Purple Pearl for the whole team. Look—Arrow is carrying the seapony flag to the starting line. Coral is on the team, too!"

The race was about to begin. But just as Arrow planted the flag, his fin tore on a jagged rock. He started to sink and was pulled into a swirling whirlpool below.

"Arrow!" cried Coral.

Before anyone else could decide what to do, Nar Wally propelled toward Arrow and jutted out his horn for the seapony to grab.

Everyone was relieved, and Coral thanked Nar Wally, but Arrow knew his injury meant big trouble for the seapony team.

"What do we do now?" asked Arrow, looking at his torn fin. "There are no other seaponies who are fast enough to race against the mermares!"

"Maybe...um...I could stand in for you?" suggested Rainbow Dash. "I've been practicing with the seaponies all day!"

"But it's the most difficult part of the race, through Crabbit's Claw Cave!" exclaimed Coral.

Electra overheard them and cried out, "There has never been a land pony in the Aquastria Race! Not that we're worried about a *land* pony beating a mermare, but it's just not done!"

King Leo made a quick decision. "I decree that Rainbow Dash may swim in Arrow's place!" he said.

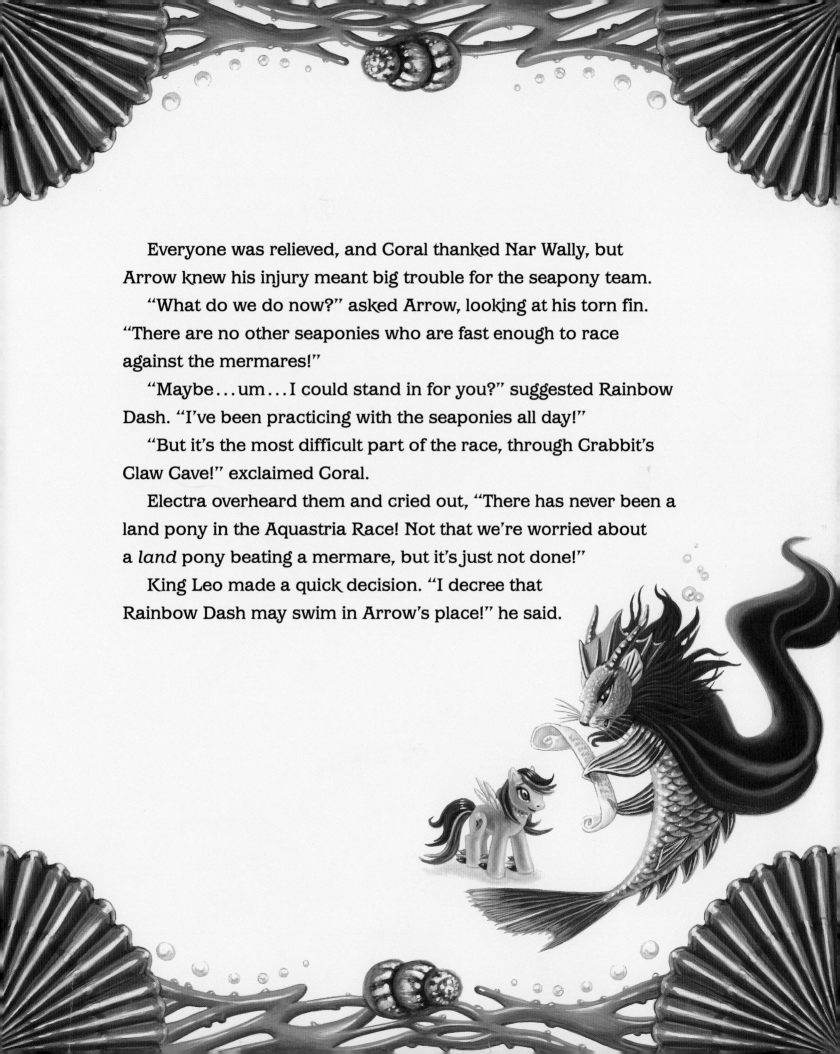

"Oh, boy, what have I gotten myself into?"
Rainbow Dash asked her friends. She was getting
nervous about racing through the cave.

"I have an idea!" Nar Wally declared.

"If you shape your tail like a fox-fin...

push your wings forward like a jellyfly...

use your hooves like a crabbit's claws...

twist your mane into a horn like mine...

and have some of Pinkie Pie's super salty-sweet seaweed snacks, then you'll definitely go faster, Rainbow Dash. Not sure how fast, but faster!"

Rainbow Dash looked determined. "Got it," she said.

The race got under way, and the seapony team was close behind the mermares. As Coral passed the shell baton to Rainbow Dash, Electra swept past her into the cave. Rainbow Dash remembered everything her friends showed her, and she pushed off with all her might.

"Can I do this?" she wondered.
Seeing the confident look on Electra's face
made Rainbow Dash decide. "I *have* to try my
best and give her some good competition!"

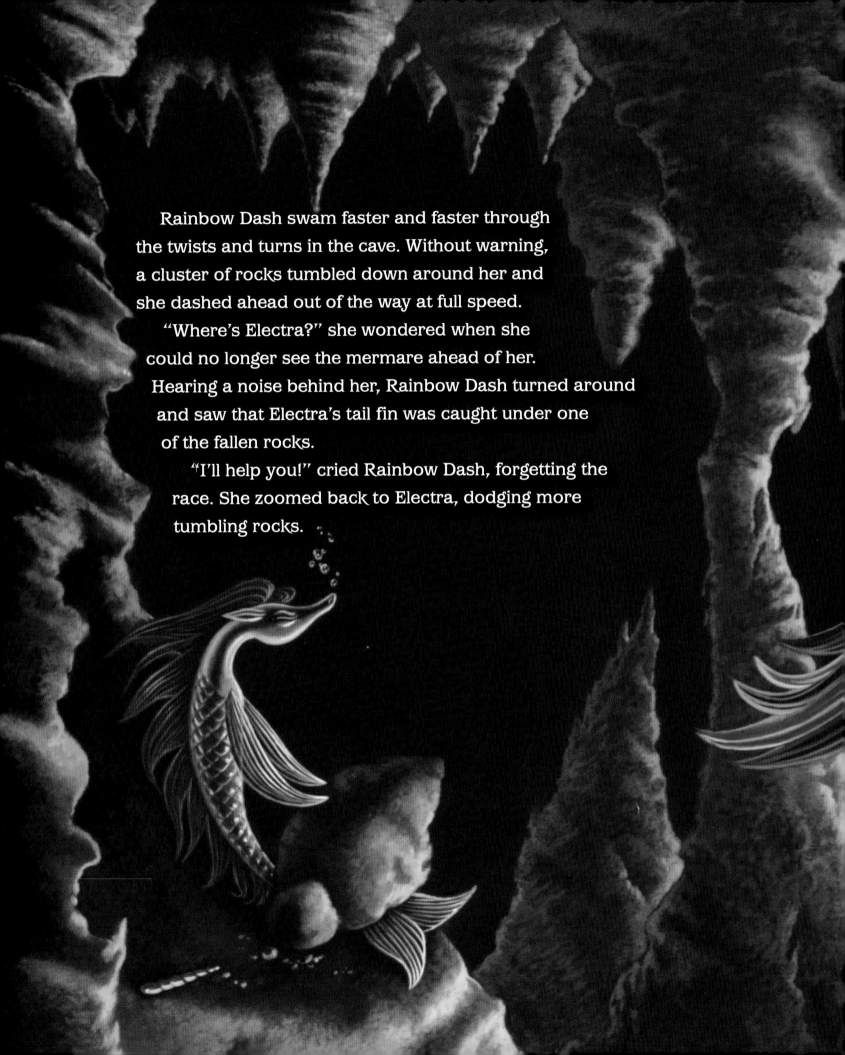

Rainbow Dash swam faster and faster through
the twists and turns in the cave. Without warning,
a cluster of rocks tumbled down around her and
she dashed ahead out of the way at full speed.

"Where's Electra?" she wondered when she
could no longer see the mermare ahead of her.
Hearing a noise behind her, Rainbow Dash turned around
and saw that Electra's tail fin was caught under one
of the fallen rocks.

"I'll help you!" cried Rainbow Dash, forgetting the
race. She zoomed back to Electra, dodging more
tumbling rocks.

After a long wait for a glimpse of the winner, the crowd outside the cave began to think there might be a problem. The ponies, Spike, and Nar Wally worried about their friend's safety.

"Do you think the little gal is okay?" asked Applejack.

"It's taking *so* long," said Rarity.

"I hope they aren't hurt!" worried Fluttershy.

Rainbow Dash and Electra finally swam out of the cave, hoof to fin. They surprised everyone as they sailed over the finish line together.

"For the first time in the history of Aquastria—*it's a tie!*" declared King Leo. Everyone cheered!

At the award ceremony that followed, Rainbow Dash and Nar Wally were given badges in honor of their bravery and kindness.

Fluttershy was so proud of both her old and her new friends. Spike was proud, too, and got so excited that he bounced too hard and nearly floated away!

Pinkie Pie brought out the giant pink kelp cake, while Rarity *ooh*ed and *aah*ed at all the fabulous fashions.

"I added the shell buttons to the ceremonial costumes. Aren't they gorgeous?" she asked Applejack.

"Nothin' is more gorgeous than a batch of freshly grown seaweed! Except maybe this here Purple Pearl," said Applejack, gazing up at the lovely prize given to the mermares and the seaponies.

Dear Princess,

Aquastria is unlike any other place I have been to! But the friends I made here are a lot like us, and I learned an important lesson about friendship today. Sometimes, helping a friend is more important than proving you're the best. We won the race together and found out that new friends are the best prize ever!

Your faithful student,
Twilight Sparkle